MySELF Bookshelf

My Best Buddy

By YeShil Kim
Illustrated by Miguel Tanco
Language Arts Consultant: Joy Cowley

NorwoodHouse Press
Chicago, Illinois

DEAR CAREGIVER

MySELF Bookshelf is a series of books that support children's social emotional learning. SEL has been proven to promote not only the development of self-awareness, responsibility, and positive relationships, but also academic achievement.

Current research reveals that the part of the brain that manages emotion is directly connected to the part of the brain that is used in cognitive tasks, such as: problem solving, logic, reasoning, and critical thinking—all of which are at the heart of learning.

SEL is also directly linked to what are referred to as 21st Century Skills: collaboration, communication, creativity, and critical thinking. MySELF Bookshelf offers an early start that will help children build the competencies for success in school and life.

In these delightful books, young children practice early reading skills while learning how to manage their own feelings and how to be considerate of other perspectives. Each book focuses on aspects of SEL that help children develop social competence that will benefit them in their relationships with others as well as in their school success. The charming characters in the stories model positive traits such as: responsibility, goal setting, determination, patience, and celebrating differences. At the end of each story, you will find a letter that highlights the positive traits and an activity or discussion to help your child apply SEL to his or her own life.

Above all, the most important part of the reading experience is to have fun and enjoy it!

Sincerely,

Shannon Cannon

Shannon Cannon, Ph.D.
Literacy and SEL Consultant

Norwood House Press • P.O. Box 316598 • Chicago, Illinois 60631
For more information about Norwood House Press please visit our website at www.norwoodhousepress.com or call 866-565-2900.

Shannon Cannon – Literacy and SEL Consultant
Joy Cowley – English Language Arts Consultant
Mary Lindeen – Consulting Editor

Paperback ISBN: 978-1-60357-693-2

The Library of Congress has cataloged the original hardcover edition with the following call number: 2014030340

Manufactured in the United States of America in Stevens Point, Wisconsin.
263N—122014

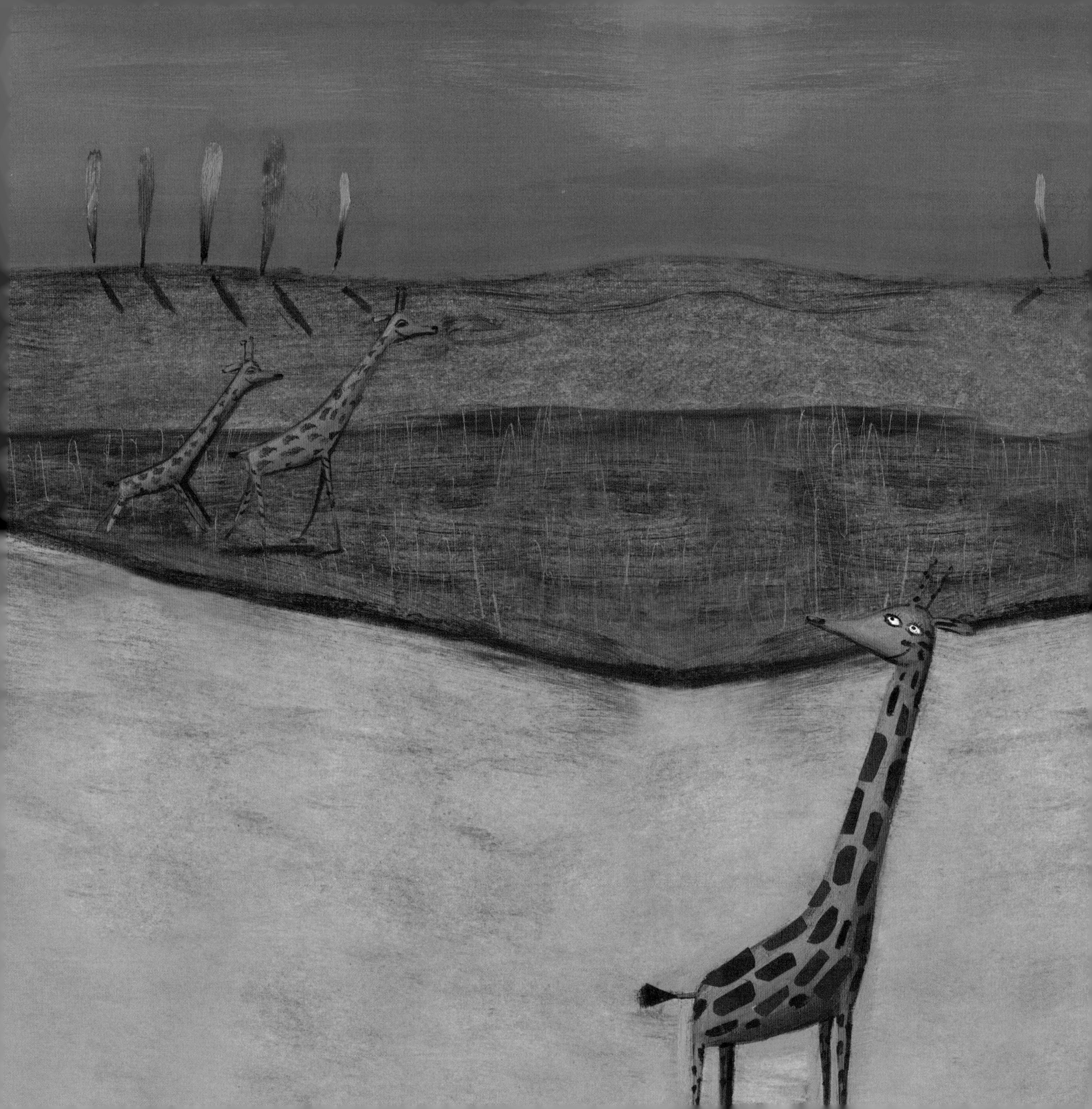

Jambo!

It means hello in Swahili.
I am Kamau and I'm in second grade.
I always say "Jambo!" to other kids
on my way to school.

They walk faster than me.
I was sick when I was little,
so I walk with a limp.
But that's okay because
I have a buddy and we walk
to school together.

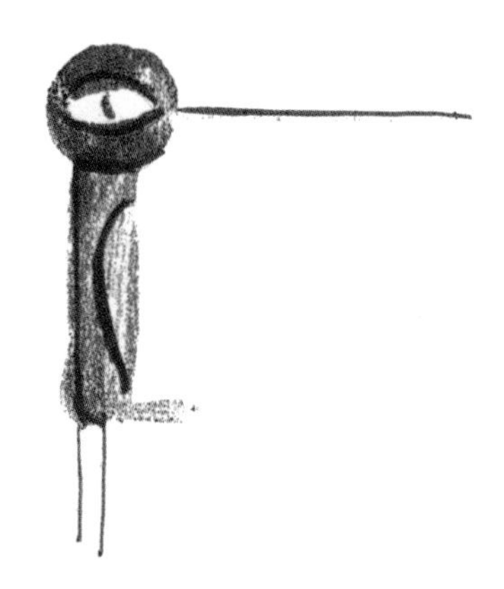

Here he comes!
My friend wears shorts and a blue jacket.
He also wears hearing aids in his ears
and he carries a cane in his hand.
He is Mamello, my best buddy.

“Jambo, Kamau!” says my friend Mamello,
and he gives me a big smile.
He does not have front teeth like me.
Mamello is eighty-five years old.
He has ten children
and thirty grandchildren.
His oldest grandson is older than my dad.
His youngest grandson is in fifth grade.
But Mamello is only in second grade.

When I go to school with Mamello,
he never tells me to walk faster.
I love talking with him on the way.
One day I asked him a question.
“Why didn’t you go to school
when you were little like me, Mamello?”

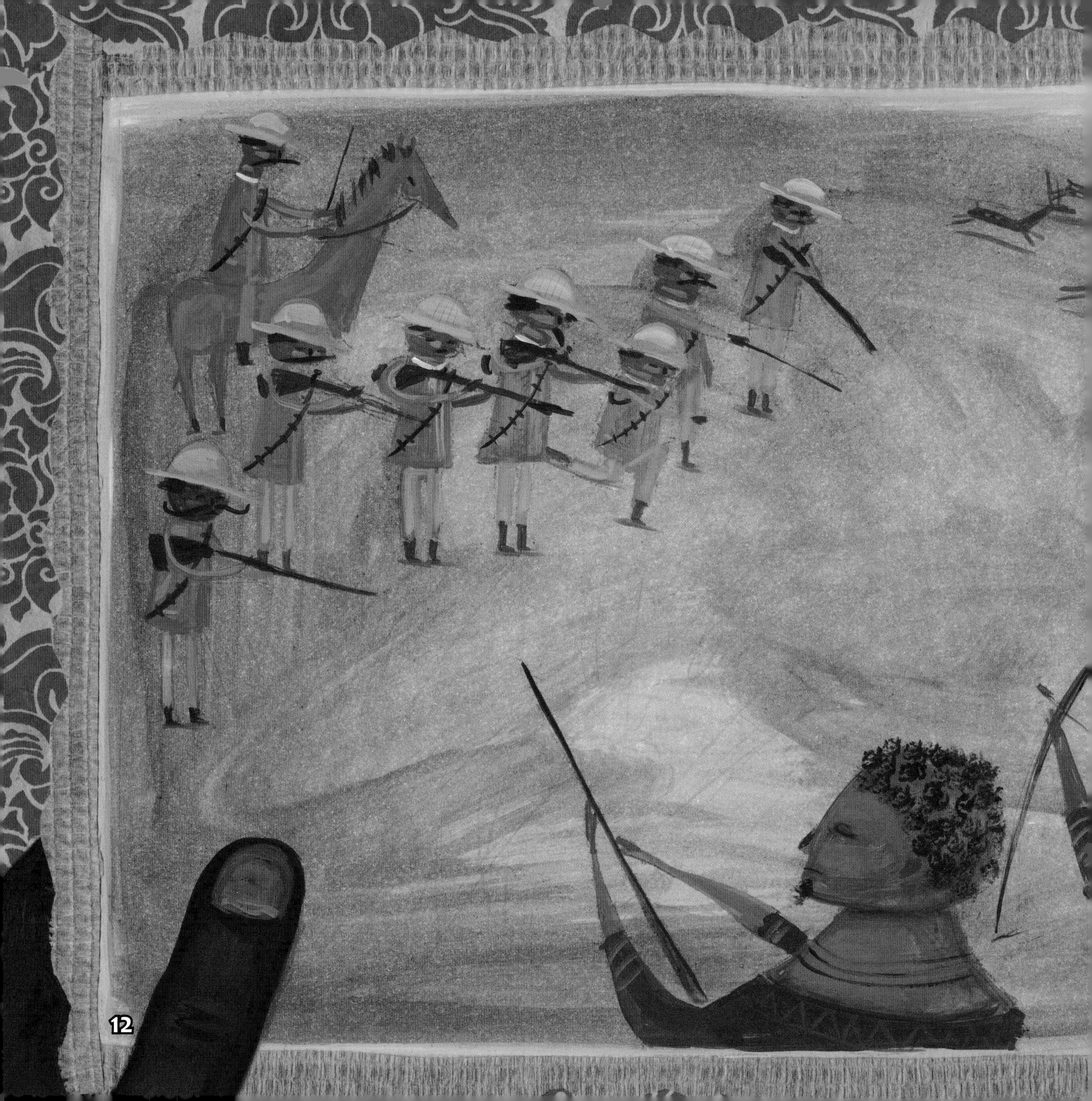

"I couldn't go to school," says Mamello.
"We were very poor,
and it was hard to find food.
We also had to fight for our country.
Some people took control,
and we had to fight to get our country back."

“Why did you want to go to school?”
I ask Mamello.

He says, “I worked on a big farm.
When I got my first paycheck
I had to write my name in a book.
I didn’t know how to write
so I just made a line in the space.
I felt very embarrassed.
Years later, I grew coffee trees
on my own land, and I dreamed
of going to school to learn how to write.”

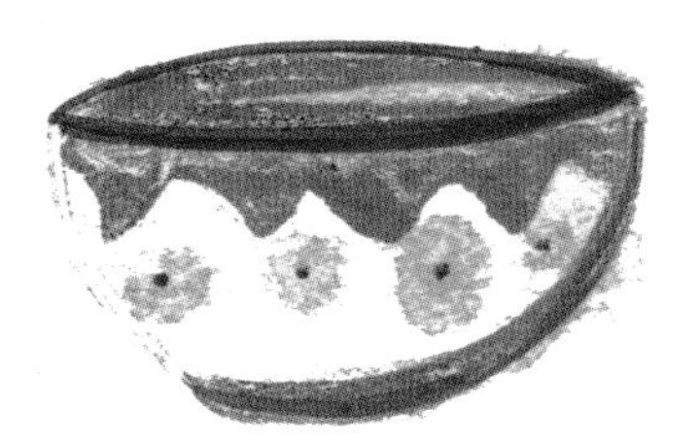

But it took a long time for Mamello's dreams to come true.
He had a big family to take care of.
He had children and then grandchildren.
His days were filled with work.
There was no time for school.

"How did you keep your dream so long?"
I ask him.

Mamello pointed to the baobab tree.
"This tree always looks dry and tough,
but when rains come to this land,
the baobab tree stores water
in its trunk and branches.
The tree is like a huge water tank.
You can store your dreams like that."

A F R I C A
28
22
30
35
25
24
32
40
ATORE
30-32
30-57

Finally, when he was eighty-four,
Mamello put down his grain sacks
and picked up a book bag.
He got some books and pencils
and left his hoe in the shed.
At last, he was going to school.

"My family worried about my age,"
he tells me, "but it is never too late
to make your dreams come true."

NAME

On his first day at school,
Mamello didn't know how to
hold a pencil correctly.
But now he can read and write well.
He also knows a lot about math
and the history of his country.

"I can write the names of my children.
I can count how many cows I have.
Learning has given me a freedom
that I didn't have before."

We are finally at the school
and I have one more question.
“Mamello, do you still have a dream?”

“Of course I do!” he tells me.
“I want to be a vet and take care
of the animals in our village.
What is your dream, Kamau?”

I point to the ostriches
that run on the grasslands.
Although they cannot fly,
they can run much faster
than any of the other birds.
They sometimes run faster
than the land animals.

“Mamello,” I say, “My dream
is to run like an ostrich.”

Jambo, Kamau!

I'm so happy that I can write
a letter to my best buddy.
Learning is an amazing thing!
I always dreamed of studying,
and now my dream has come true.
My new dream is to become a vet.
The great thing about dreams
is that they give us hope for tomorrow.
Kamau, do not give up on your dreams.
Remember to keep on trying
to make your dreams come true.

From,
Your best buddy Mamello

SOCIAL AND EMOTIONAL LEARNING FOCUS

Pursuing One's Dream

Mamello always kept hope that his dreams would come true, no matter how long it took. He told Kamau that he could store his dreams just like the baobab tree stores water in its trunk and branches.

You can make a tree to store your dreams!

- Ask an adult to save you a cardboard roll when the paper towels are all used.
- Cut the straight lines ½ inch apart, from the top of the roll, about 4 inches down.
- Bend the cut "strips" to form branches.
- Use markers or paint to make the roll look like the bark on a tree.
- You can make a bark-like texture by crinkling a piece of a brown grocery bag and gluing it on to the roll.
- Write each of your dreams on different "leaves" cut out from colored paper
- Attach the leaves to the branches on your tree.

Do you know that you can have friends who are much older than you, just like Kamau? There may be a senior citizen center near your home. The residents may have families who live far away. They would love for you to visit and talk, read, sing, and play games. They can tell you stories about their dreams, and you can share your own. Ask your parents to see if there is one near you. If you cannot visit in person, you can find a pen pal and write letters or emails to each other.

Reader's Theater

Reader's Theater is an interactive approach to reading that allows students to understand each story through dramatic interpretation. By involving students in reading, listening, and speaking activities, they provide an integrated approach for students to develop fluency and comprehension. A Reader's Theater edition of this book is available online. You can access the script by scanning the QR code to the right or visit our website at:
http://www.norwoodhousepress.com/mybestbuddy.aspx

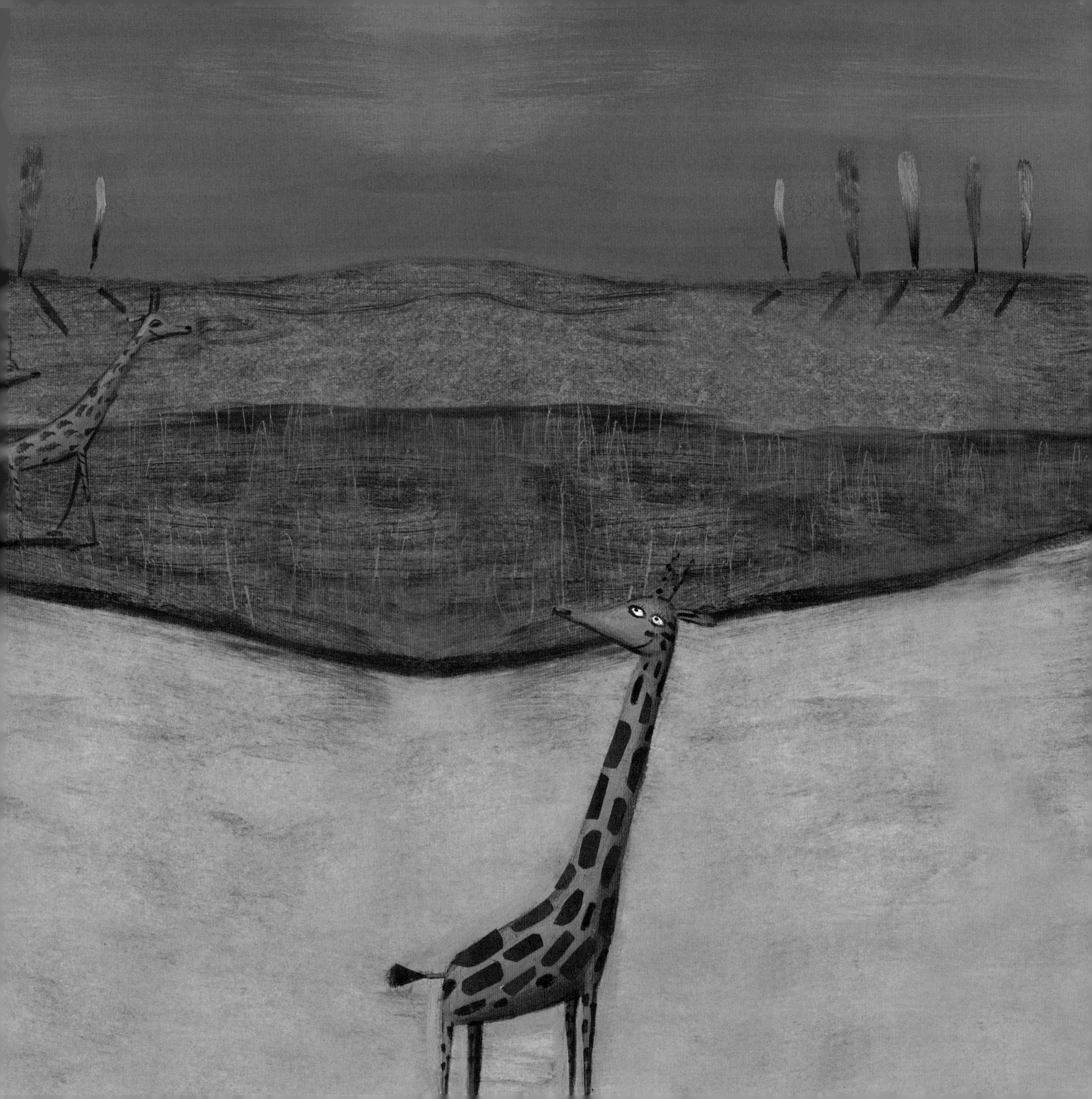